Witches Do Not Like Bicycles

For my nephew Eoin Hopwood with all my love,

and with thanks to Aideen Molloy for Mrs Beasly.

P.F.

To Julie and Fanny, two supergirls

who rock the world!

J.D.

EGMONT

We bring stories to life

Book Band: Purple

First published in Great Britain 2014
This Reading Ladder edition published 2016
by Egmont UK Limited
The Yellow Building, 1 Nicholas Road, London W11 4AN
Text copyright © Patricia Forde 2014
Illustrations copyright © Joëlle Dreidemy 2014
The author and illustrator have asserted their moral rights
ISBN 978 1 4052 8218 5
www.egmont.co.uk
A CIP catalogue record for this title is available from the British Library.
Printed in Singapore
57031/2

Series consultant: Nikki Gamble

Witches Do Not Like Bicycles

Patricia Forde and Joëlle Dreidemy

Reading Ladder

I broke my leg last summer, the day
after my birthday.

I had to stay in my bed, at the top of
the house, for a whole week.

Lola, my sister, played in the garden under my window. I could hear her, though I couldn't see her.

'Natalie!' she called one afternoon.

'Yes, Lola,' I said.

'Natalie!' she said. 'You must be SO
bored . . .'

'No,' I said. 'I have a good book
and –'

'Well, don't worry, Natalie,' Lola said,
ignoring me. 'My friend Mrs Beasly
is coming round to play, and she is
GREAT fun. I'm going to make sure
you don't miss a thing.'

7

Mrs Beasly is Lola's latest friend. An invisible friend. Not invisible to Lola, but invisible to the rest of us.

'Do you think that's a good idea, Lola?' I said. 'Mrs Beasly caused a lot of trouble last time she was here . . .'

A stone flew through the window and landed on the floor of my room. There was a string tied around the stone.

I pulled on the string and up came one half of the walkie-talkie Nan bought me for my birthday.

Lola's voice crackled at the other end.
'Lola?' I said. 'What are you doing with my walkie-talkie?'
'Natalie! I can't talk now. Mrs Beasly has just arrived and she's brought her dog, Pebbles!'

'Her dog?' I said, sitting up. 'What
kind of a dog?'

'Only a baby one,' Lola said. 'And he is
SO cute! Oh . . . oh no!'

'What?' I said. 'What's happening,
Lola?'

'Ah . . . nothing to worry about Natalie,' Lola said. 'It's just that Pebbles saw your bike, and he is trying to cycle it. It's very funny really.'

'My new bike? My brand new bike that

I only got to ride on once?!'

Lola said nothing.

'DAD!' I yelled.

'It's OK, Natalie,' Lola said. 'He's cycling very nicely now, though he just ran over the elephant's toe . . .'

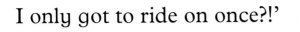

Ding-a-ling!

'Elephant?'

'A huge elephant, Natalie. I wish you could see her . . . She's called Rosie,' Lola said. 'Oh dear! Rosie just sucked

up all the water from the fountain and she's squirting it at Pebbles.'

splooooosh!

The fountain!

'Take my bike away from that fountain!' I said. 'Lola! Do you hear me? It will only get rusty. Lola?'

Are you there?

Just then, Dad put his head round the door.

'Be with you in a minute, Natalie,' he said. I'm just calling the plumber. Problem with the fountain in the garden. Water everywhere . . .'

'But Dad –' I said, just before he disappeared.

Lola was still talking.

'Don't worry about the elephant,
Natalie,' she said. 'There isn't any
more water left now.'

Everything is under control.

I could hardly get the words out.

'Dad!' I yelled.

Dad came running in again.

'Are you all right, darling?' he said,
his face all worried.

'No!' I said. 'I'm not all right!
There's a dog riding my bike and an
an elephant in the garden and . . . you
have to do something!'

'Oh dear,' Dad said. 'I think you have a fever. I'll call the doctor.'

'No!' I said. 'It's not a fever, it's a DOG and an ELEPHANT!'

But Dad was gone. I sank back
on my pillows, exhausted. Just then the
walkie-talkie came to life again.

'Oh, Natalie! As well as the dog and the elephant, Mrs Beasly's got a pig called Grunty . . .' Lola said.

oink
oink

'Grunty is letting me stroke her head as long as I let her play with Mum's dress.'

'You are letting a pig play with Mum's dress?'

'It was on the clothes line, Natalie, and it's nice to share. I'm sure Mum wouldn't mind. Did I tell you that Mrs Beasly used to be in the circus?'

'No, you didn't,' I said crossly.

'She was a tightrope walker,' said Lola.

'Really?' I said. 'What's happening to my bike?'

'That's all sorted now. Pebbles and
Rosie are friends again and –'

'What about my bike?' I said.

'Ah . . . I can't see your bike . . .
Mrs Beasly! Mrs Beasly!'

I was getting desperate.

'Where is my bike, Lola? Where is it?'

'Oh,' Lola said. 'Mrs Beasly says it's

missing presumed stolen.'

'Stolen?' I said. 'STOLEN? Who
would steal my BRAND NEW bike?'

'That is a good question, Natalie,
and we are going to find the answer.
Mrs Beasly used to be a detective,
you know.'

Hmmm . . .

'But you said she used to be a
tightrope walker.'
'Hush!' said Lola, ignoring me.
'We are looking for clues.'

There was silence for a moment, then I heard Lola again.

'Aha!'

'Aha?' I said, feeling rather weak.

'Aha!' Lola repeated. 'We just found a pointy black hat tossed in the gooseberry bushes . . .'

'Whose hat?' I said.

'Mrs Beasly suspects . . . Rubella the
Witch!'

'Mrs Beasly thinks that some silly old
witch has taken my bike?' I said slowly.
'Why would she do that? Why would
a witch –'

With that, Dad appeared again, with a
hammer in his hands.

'Back soon, Natalie. The clothes line
just fell down. Need to fix it before
your mum gets home.'

'Aagh!' Lola shrieked in my ear. 'There she is!'

'Who?' I moaned.

'Rubella the Witch . . . on your bike.'

'No!' I said.

'Yes!' said Lola. 'Mrs Beasly is chasing her on Rosie's back.

Ooooh!

Aaaaaah!

Oops . . . she nearly
fell off. Oh no!'
'Oh no?' I said.
'Rubella has put a spell on Pebbles
and turned him into . . .

'. . . a mouse! Elephants are terrified
of mice, as you know, and Rosie just
stood on her back legs and knocked
Mrs Beasly right off. But wait . . .'

'Yes?' I said, almost falling out of my bed.

'Mrs Beasly just jumped up on the clothes line and is running across it with an umbrella in one hand!'

Another silence, then
more crackling and
I heard Lola again.
'Oh good for Mrs
Beasly! She just
jumped off the line and knocked
Rubella off your bike.'

'My bike,' I managed to say. 'Is my bike all right?'

Lola laughed.

'Oh look!' she said. 'Mrs Beasly has just turned Pebbles back into Pebbles.

And Grunty is chasing Rubella all over
the garden!'

'Is my bike all right?' I yelled into the
walkie-talkie.

snort

'Now, now, Natalie!'
Lola said calmly.
'Your bike is just
fine, but you
mustn't get too
excited. I know how bored
you are, but the doctor said you
needed to rest.'
'What's happened to the witch?' I said.
'Mmm . . .' said Lola, 'Mrs Beasly says
that witches do not like bicycles.'

'Don't they?'
I gasped.

43

'No. They prefer broomsticks.
See! Rubella just flew right past your
window . . .'

I looked towards the window, but I couldn't see anything.

Just then, Dad came in with the doctor.

'Now, Natalie!' he said, taking out his stethoscope. 'How are you today?'
The walkie-talkie crackled beside me. 'Goodbye, Mrs Beasly!' I heard Lola say. 'Goodbye Rosie! Goodbye! Goodbye Grunty!'

Goodbye! Goodbye!

'Phew!' I said. 'I feel a lot better now.'

'You do?' the doctor said, raising an eyebrow.

'Yes,' I said. 'I feel a lot better now that

I know that . . .

Witches Do Not
Like Bicycles,